Alex and the Box Shop

The Sound of X

by Cecilia Minden and Joanne Meier • illustrated by Bob Ostrom

The Child's World

Published by The Child's World®
1980 Lookout Drive
Mankato, MN 56003-1705
800-599-READ
www.childsworld.com

The Child's World®: Mary Berendes, Publishing Director
The Design Lab: Design and page production

Library of Congress Cataloging-in-Publication Data
Minden, Cecilia.
  Alex and the box shop : the sound of X / by Cecilia
Minden and Joanne Meier ; illustrated by Bob Ostrom.
    p. cm.
  ISBN 978-1-60253-422-3 (library bound : alk. paper)
  1. English language—Consonants—Juvenile literature.
  2. English language—Phonetics—Juvenile literature. 3.
Reading—Phonetic method—Juvenile literature. I. Meier,
Joanne D. II. Ostrom, Bob. III. Title.
  PE1159.M5623 2010
  [E]—dc22   2010005611

Printed in the United States of America in Mankato, MN.
July 2010
F11538

NOTE TO PARENTS AND EDUCATORS:

The Child's World® has created this series with the goal of exposing children to engaging stories and illustrations that assist in phonics development. The books in the series will help children learn the relationships between the letters of written language and the individual sounds of spoken language. This contact helps children learn to use these relationships to read and write words.

The books in this series follow a similar format. An introductory page, to be read by an adult, introduces the child to the phonics feature, or sound, that will be highlighted in the book. Read this page to the child, stressing the phonic feature. Help the student learn how to form the sound with her mouth. The story and engaging illustrations follow the introduction. At the end of the story, word lists categorize the feature words into their phonic elements.

Each book in this series has been carefully written to meet specific readability requirements. Close attention has been paid to elements such as word count, sentence length, and vocabulary. Readability formulas measure the ease with which the text can be read and understood. Each book in this series has been analyzed using the Spache readability formula.

Reading research suggests that systematic phonics instruction can greatly improve students' word recognition, spelling, and comprehension skills. This series assists in the teaching of phonics by providing students with important opportunities to apply their knowledge of phonics as they read words, sentences, and text.

This is the letter x.

In this book, you will read words that have the **x** sound as in: *excited, box, fox,* and *six.*

Alex is excited.

He is in Uncle Max's shop.

Uncle Max sells boxes.

Alex puts the boxes in piles.

Little boxes go in one pile.

Big boxes go in another pile.

People come in to buy boxes.

Mr. Cox comes into the shop. He needs a box for a toy fox.

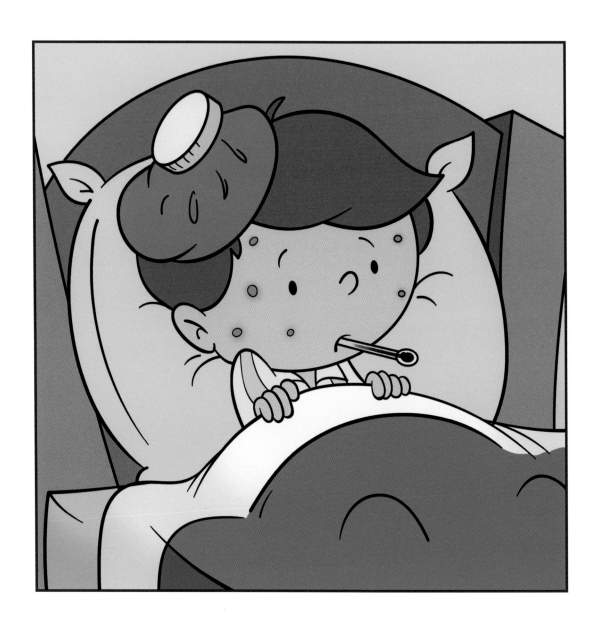

The fox is for his son Rex.

Rex has the chicken pox.

Mrs. Baxter comes in next.

She needs a big box
for Roxy. Roxy is
Mrs. Baxter's cat.

Why does Roxy need a big box? Roxy just had six kittens!

Fun Facts

Chicken pox is a disease that spreads easily. You can get chicken pox at any age, but patients are usually between two and six years old. Once you are exposed to chicken pox, it takes about two weeks for the red, itchy bumps to appear. You may run a fever. If you've had chicken pox once, you probably won't catch it again. A shot from your doctor may help you avoid catching chicken pox.

A male fox is known as a dog. A female fox is called a vixen, and a baby fox is called a kit. Foxes are found on every continent except Antarctica. There are more than 25 different types of foxes. Some foxes can live to be 14 years old.

Activity

Building a Box Village
Gather boxes of different shapes and sizes to create your village. Begin with the largest boxes on the bottom and add the medium-sized boxes next. The smallest boxes should be on the top. You can tape or glue them together as you build. If you want your village to be colorful, cover your boxes with construction paper before you begin. Make sure to add windows and doors to your buildings!

To Learn More

Books
About the Sound of X
Moncure, Jane Belk. *My "x" Sound Box®*. Mankato, MN: The Child's World, 2009.

About Boxes
Fleming, Candace, and Stacey Dressen-McQueen (illustrator). *Boxes for Katje*. New York: Farrar, Straus and Giroux, 2003.
Morrison, Toni, Slade Morrison, and Giselle Potter (illustrator). *The Big Box*. New York: Hyperion Books for Children, 1999.

About Chicken Pox
Dealey, Erin, and Hanako Wakiyama (illustrator). *Goldie Locks Has Chicken Pox*. New York: Atheneum Books for Young Readers, 2002.
Maccarone, Grace, and Besty Lewin (illustrator). *Itchy, Itchy Chicken Pox*. New York: Scholastic, 1992.

About Foxes
Markle, Sandra. *Foxes*. Minneapolis, MN: Lerner Publications, 2009.
Royston, Angela, and Jane Burton. *Fox*. New York: DK Publishing, 2008.
Spilsbury, Louise. *Foxes*. Chicago, IL: Raintree, 2010.

Web Sites
Visit our home page for lots of links about the Sound of X:

childsworld.com/links

Note to Parents, Teachers, and Librarians: We routinely check our Web links to make sure they're safe, active sites—so encourage your readers to check them out!

X Feature Words

Proper Names
Alex
Baxter
Cox
Max
Rex
Roxy

Feature Words in Medial Position
excited
next

Feature Words in Final Position
box
fox
pox
six

About the Authors

Cecilia Minden, PhD, is the former director of the Language and Literacy Program at the Harvard Graduate School of Education. She is now a reading consultant for school and library publications. She earned her PhD in reading education from the University of Virginia. Cecilia and her husband, Dave Cupp, live outside Chapel Hill, North Carolina. They enjoy sharing their love of reading with their grandchildren, Chelsea and Qadir.

Joanne Meier, PhD, has worked as an elementary school teacher, university professor, and researcher. She earned her BA in early childhood education from the University of South Carolina, and her MEd and PhD in education from the University of Virginia. She currently works as a literacy consultant for schools and private organizations. Joanne lives in Virginia with her husband Eric, daughters Kella and Erin, two cats, and a gerbil.

About the Illustrator

Bob Ostrom has been illustrating children's books for nearly twenty years. A graduate of the New England School of Art & Design at Suffolk University, Bob has worked for such companies as Disney, Nickelodeon, and Cartoon Network. He lives in North Carolina with his wife Melissa and three children, Will, Charlie, and Mae.